YOU CAN CALL ME WILLY

A Story for Children About AIDS

by Joan C. Verniero

illustrated by Verdon Flory

Magination Press

Library of Congress Cataloging-in-Publication Data

Verniero, Joan.
  You can call me Willy : a story for children about AIDS / by Joan
C. Verniero ; illustrated by Verdon Flory.
      p.   cm.
  Summary: Although eight-year-old Willy has AIDS, she wants to play
baseball.
    ISBN 0-945354-60-6
    [1. Aids (Disease)–Fiction. 2. Baseball–Fiction.
  3. Friendship–Fiction. 4. Afro-Americans–Fiction.] I. Flory,
Verdon, ill. II. Title.
  PZ7.V5975Yo 1995
  [E]–dc20   94-13074
                                                          CIP
                                                           AC

Published by
Magination Press
An Educational Publishing Foundation Book
American Psychological Association
750 First Street, NE
Washington, DC 20002

Manufactured in the United States of America.

10 9 8 7 6 5 4 3 2

INTRODUCTION FOR PARENTS

Based on the experiences of an eight-year-old girl, *You Can Call Me Willy* is designed to help young children understand more about AIDS.

The book avoids supplying too many facts, which can scare young children and alienate them from the character of Willy. AIDS transmission is treated on a level appropriate to children between the ages of four and eight. That the virus is contracted through the blood is addressed so parents, educators, or mental health professionals can elaborate if they feel it appropriate to do so. The book explains that Willy contracted HIV at birth because her mother was infected. It does not mention, however, that Willy's mother contracted HIV as an IV-drug user. Depending on the readiness of the youngsters reading the book, parents and professionals can teach that HIV is spread through sexual intercourse, the birth canal, contaminated needles and, until the mid-1980s in the US, contaminated blood transfusions.

Through the story, parents and professionals can focus on how difficult a virus HIV is to catch. They can allay children's fears that AIDS is transmitted through inanimate objects. Most importantly, adults can teach youngsters that children with HIV and AIDS cannot transmit the virus by being in the same class or playing the same games as uninfected children.

The story teaches how a child with HIV feels about being alive. Willy chooses not to think about the fact that she will probably die. Like all children, what she wants is to have friends, go to school and play. From the particulars of how Willy copes with her illness, adults can further discuss with their own children what it means for a child to have HIV.

Another objective of the book is to encourage compassion toward children with HIV and AIDS. Children with AIDS are still children. As uninfected children hear and read Willy's thoughts about how she feels and looks, they can see themselves in her place on days when they feel that they don't belong. Uninfected youngsters will develop an understanding that children with HIV and AIDS share the same desires and face many of the same difficulties they do.

Children who are infected with HIV or AIDS should find comfort in the character of Willy. They will see how she copes with her illness and where she finds strength. HIV-infected children should find it rewarding that another HIV-infected child can face adversity and find a satisfactory solution.

To Erica and Willy for their inspiration
and to Christine Leahy-Keenan
for her medical expertise

—JCV

I was named Wilhelmina Jones. I was eight in September. My friends call me Willy. You can call me Willy, too.

I live with my grandma. I call my grandma Mommy. Everybody else calls her my mommy, too. She's the only mother I remember.

Mommy reminds me to wear extra clothes when I go outside. I put on a sweater, socks and jeans, even in the summer.

I have the virus that causes AIDS. The virus is called HIV.

It's not easy to catch HIV and get AIDS. You have to get the virus into your blood first. Many children like me got HIV from their mothers when they were born.

Mommy has taken care of me since I was a baby.

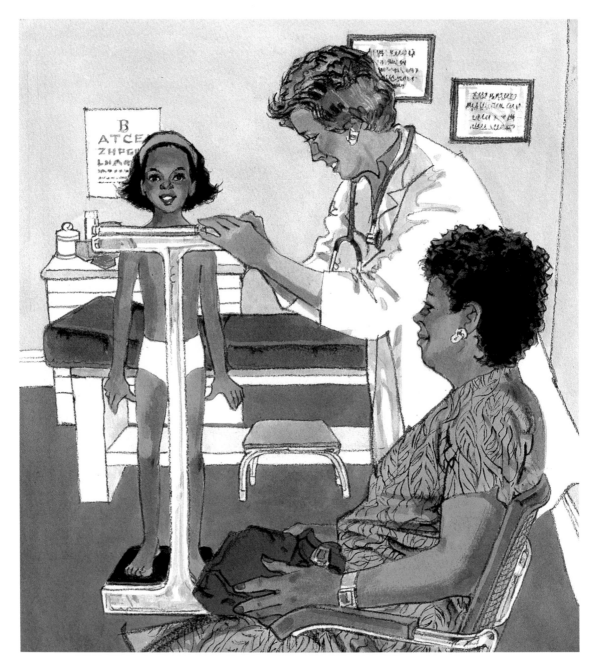

At the clinic, I see Doctor Christine. When we first met, Doctor Christine said I was too skinny. She taught Mommy and me about foods that will make me fatter and won't hurt my stomach.

My favorite lunch is a banana and sesame butter sandwich.
Mommy mixes a powder into my milk to make me gain weight.

Dexter Demie is my best friend. He lives right next door, and we are both in the third grade at Huckleberry Hill School.

Dexter brings me the homework when I am too sick to go to school.

My medicine keeps me strong. At home, Mommy gives me lots of pills. At school, Ms. Jeffries, the nurse, gives them to me.

I've had many kinds of medicine. Some make my cheeks puff out. The pills I take now taste better than the syrup I used to take.

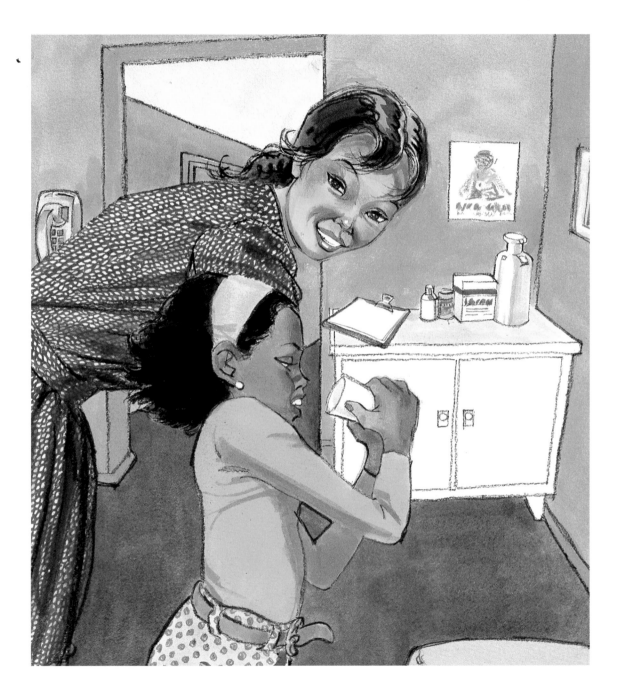

Before I could go to Huckleberry Hill, Mommy had to prove I would not make anybody sick. Mommy brought notes from the clinic to Huckleberry Hill. She took doctors and lawyers and social workers to meetings with her.

They told the parents nobody catches AIDS from toilet seats or doorknobs. They talked about how kids won't get AIDS from my sweat or saliva. They also showed the teachers what to do if I get a cut.

Some days, I have to stay away from Dexter and from school, even when I feel good.

Mommy says I could die if I catch viruses and infections from the kids at school. I don't heal fast like the other kids.

It's hard for me to think about dying from AIDS. What I like to think about are happy things like school and baseball.

I'm glad I feel good this year. It means I have more days to play

with Dexter. Dexter is the best hitter in the whole school.

Some kids at Huckleberry Hill still stare. Some girls tease me about my clothes, like when I wear tights, and they think it's too hot outside. Some kids think I look funny, because I'm still losing my baby teeth.

I tell the kids who tease me that I'm special. I tell them it's cool to look different.

Bettina Marks is the one person in my class who almost made my life miserable. Bettina came to Huckleberry Hill from another state a month ago.

The Friday after she came to school was the day to sign up for summer baseball. When Bettina saw me go up to the table to sign my name, she said, "Willy has AIDS!" She said it really loud, so everybody could hear her.

The coach said, "Willy's doctor says she can play baseball. That's fine with me."

"How do I know Bettina is safe?" Bettina's father asked.

"No one catches AIDS from a baseball bat, Mr. Marks," said the coach. "Why don't you visit the school nurse tomorrow to learn about HIV and AIDS?"

I was speechless, which was unusual for me. But Dexter spoke up. "Willy's my best friend. If Willy doesn't play baseball, neither do I." Mommy hugged Dexter and me. Her arm around my back was strong. I let the good feeling pass through me.

"It's okay, kids," said the coach to me and Dexter. "You'll both play. Everyone who signs up for Little League will play."

"Let's go home and practice, Willy," Dexter said.
"Cool!" I said. Then I told him I was glad he was my best friend.

RESOURCES

AIDS National Interfaith Network (ANIN), 110 Maryland Avenue, N.E., Suite 504, Washington, DC 20002; (202) 546-0807

AIDS Resource Foundation for Children, 182 Roseville Avenue, Newark, NJ 07107; (201) 483-4250

American Civil Liberties Union AIDS Project, 132 West 43rd Street, Box NEP, New York, NY 10036; (212) 944-9800, ext. 545

AmFAR (American Foundation for AIDS Research), 1828 L Street, NW, Suite 802, Washington, DC 20036; (202) 331-8606

Department of Health & Human Services, Public Health Service, National Institutes of Health, Building 10, Room 13N240, Bethesda, MD 20892

GMHC (Gay Men's Health Crisis), 129 West 20th Street, New York, NY 10011; Hotline: (212) 807-6655

National AIDS Hotline, (800) 342-AIDS; Spanish Access: (800) 342-AIDS; Spanish Access: (800) 344-SIDA; Deaf Access, TTY/TDD: (800) 243-7889

National AIDS Information Clearinghouse (NAIC), (800) 458-5231; Deaf Access, TTY/TDD: (800) 243-7012

National Pediatric HIV Resource Center Hotline, Children's Hospital of New Jersey, 15 South Ninth Street, Newark, NJ 07107; (201) 268-8251

The Orphan Project, 121 Avenue of the Americas, 6th Floor, New York, NY 10013; (212) 925-5290

U.S. Conference of Mayors, "Local HIV Policies Resource Guide," 1620 I Street, NW, Washington, DC 20006; (202) 293-7330